THE SEEKERS

HARI & DEEPTI

Alfred A. Knopf   New York

THIS IS A BORZOI BOOK PUBLISHED BY ALFRED A. KNOPF

Visit us on the Web! rhcbooks.com

Educators and librarians, for a variety of teaching tools, visit us at RHTeachersLibrarians.com

Library of Congress Cataloging-in-Publication Data
Names: Panicker, Hari, author, illustrator. | Nair, Deepti, author, illustrator.
Title: The Seekers / Hari & Deepti.
Description: First edition. | New York : Alfred A. Knopf, [2019] | Summary: Siblings Mio and Nao learn that the old stories of spirits are true
when they lead a group of villagers to find out what is stopping the river. Features backlit papercut illustrations.
Identifiers: LCCN 2017003437 | ISBN 978-1-5247-0152-9 (trade) | ISBN 978-1-5247-0153-6 (lib. bdg.) | ISBN 978-1-5247-0154-3 (ebook)
Subjects: | CYAC: Spirituality—Fiction. | Villages—Fiction. | Environmental protection—Fiction.
Classification: LCC PZ7.1.P35744 See 2018 | DDC [E]—dc23

The text of this book is set in 17-point Bembo Book.
The illustrations were created using hand-cut colored paper with backlighting, which is photographed and digitally edited.

MANUFACTURED IN CHINA
August 2019

10   9   8   7   6   5   4   3   2   1

First Edition

This book is dedicated to our family and friends
who selflessly supported us through our art journey.
Thank you!

In the valley of Krum, legend has it that the land was guarded by the spirits of Ice and Fire— the Silver Fox and the Fire Wolf.

They were two halves of a whole.
Day & Night.
Ice & Fire.

But that was a long time ago.
No one has seen them in years, and they
exist only in stories told by the village elders.

Now when the river recedes every morning,
the villagers forage the forest floor for the
crown-shell snails, the key ingredient in their delicious soup.

As the night pulls its dark blanket of stars
over the valley, the river flows back and the villagers
return to their homes among the treetops.

Life is calm.

On the tallest tree live siblings Mio and Nao.

They are brave and they are fierce.

They are the best gatherers in all of Krum.

Nao is a dreamer with a wanderer's soul. She is fearless at heart and longs to climb the distant mountains.

One day, she did wander off to the edge of the valley. There she found
buried in the swamp a unique crown-shell snail. Inside the shell was a
beautiful jewel, which shone like the night sky, full of stars.
She tied it around her neck. "It has magic!" she cried.

Mio feels otherwise. He thinks things have been different since the day
Nao found the jewel. The sky is darker. The river has changed. Each night
the water returns slower and slower. There have been fewer shells to gather.

"Something is not right."

Then, just as he feared, the river left the valley and
never returned. A day passed and then two, and the snails
started to die. The valley was in danger.

Mio told the villagers, "I fear the guardian spirits have
abandoned Krum forever." The villagers scoffed at him,
but Nao suggested that they should travel beyond the valley
and find what was stopping the river.

"But no one has ever left the valley," said a villager.

Even so, other villagers—Kai, Toma, and Kaya—
volunteered to join them on their quest into the unknown.

As they traveled, they found that what once
had been a raging river was now quiet and grim.
They found lifeless trees and smoke-filled skies.

Eventually the river disappeared into deep caverns
they could have once only imagined.

The others grew weary and anxious about
these strange sights. They wanted to head back home.
On the verge of giving up, they spotted a glow in the distance.

They were drawn to it as if under a spell.

They could hardly contain their excitement when they
came upon a trove of glittery jewels.
"This would look good on my tree."
"No, that one's mine."
"I spotted it first."
"Stop! Please stop!" Mio cried in disbelief.

He reminded them of their mission.
And their families back home.
The others grumbled, but agreed to go on when
Nao was struck with an idea.
"We should follow the trail of jewels. Perhaps it
will lead us to something we need."
And so they continued on.

When they emerged from the caverns,
an eerie orange light surrounded them. Smoke was billowing
on the horizon. People were fleeing the flames in panic.

"What happened?" Nao asked a villager

"We were foolish. We cut down and burned trees to fuel our greed.

Then the Fire Wolf appeared and his fury destroyed everything.
Soon there will be nothing left. Our land is doomed."

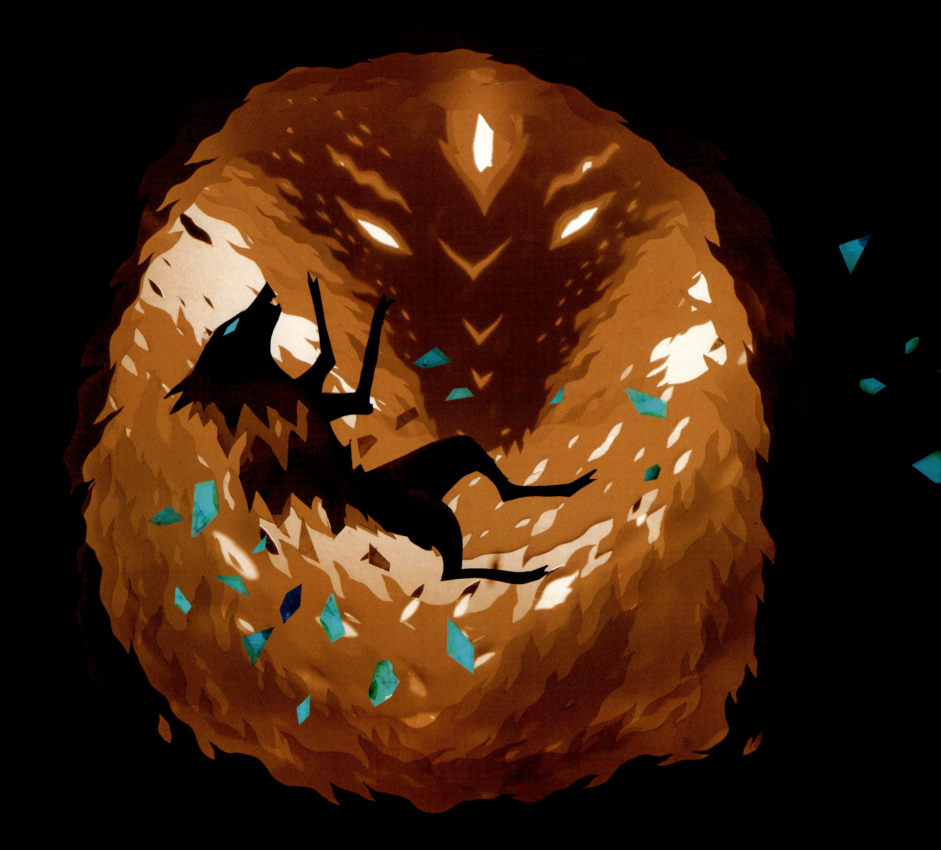

Mio had known all along that the legends were true. But how had the Fire Wolf become so powerful? Where was the Silver Fox?

Suddenly it all made sense! *The jewels!* They were once the Silver Fox, destroyed by the villagers' actions.

"We must revive the Silver Fox. Gather all the jewels. It might be the only way to stop the Wolf."

Reluctantly, Kai, Toma, and Kaya laid down their jewels and began to fit the pieces together, but the Fox still did not rise.

With the Wolf's rage quelled and the Fox
back to its full strength, harmony was restored
and the river began to flow again.

On their journey home to Krum, they could
finally take in the beauty of the wider world

Krum welcomed them as heroes.
"Cheers to the Seekers!"

Mio and Nao are still the best gatherers.
And now they are on the lookout for their
next adventure.

AUTHORS' NOTE

Our art has always explored the complex relationship between humans and their surroundings and has a constant theme of discovery and coexistence.

Born in cities, we are always in a struggle with nature and have often witnessed mountains and forests consumed to make way for high-rises. The consequences of which we have now started to see, with changing weather patterns and other calamities like floods, droughts, and wildfires.

We wanted to address this issue through our art and storytelling. *The Seekers* follows the inhabitants of a peaceful village who lose one of their most precious resources—water—because of the actions of a neighboring village upstream. The Seekers must search for answers and soon discover the wider world as they come face to face with their fears.

The story explores how our actions may have untoward consequences, which can be addressed with awareness of, and respect for, our planet and its resources.

We put careful thought into every page of this book, which was created over the course of two years, in three countries, and which took thirty handmade dioramas, over 600 layers of cut paper, and countless paper cuts to bring to fruition.

We hope you love this book as much as we loved making it.

HARI & DEEPTI